MOOSE on the LOOSE

To my friends at Washington School,

I enjoyed my visit to your school and sharing my books with you. I hope the missing moose gives you lots of laughs.

Happy reading,

Carol Partridge Ochs

MOOSE on the LOOSE

by Carol Partridge Ochs

Illustrations by Anastasia Mitchell

Carolrhoda Books, Inc./Minneapolis

For Fred
—C.P.O.

To my mother, Anna Marie Moore,
for her support and
encouragement   —A.M.

Copyright © 1991 by Carolrhoda Books, Inc.

Library of Congress Cataloging-in-Publication Data

Ochs, Carol Partridge.
Moose on the loose / by Carol Partridge Ochs ; illustrated by
Anastasia Mitchell.
p.   cm.
Summary: A zookeeper and a railroad man acquire more and more
helpers as they search the town for a lost moose and a missing
caboose.
ISBN 0-87614-448-2
[1. Moose—Fiction. 2. Railroads—Trains—Fiction. 3. Humorous
stories.] I. Mitchell, Anastasia, ill. II. Title.
PZ7.0167Mo 1991
[E]—dc20   90-35235
                                                CIP
                                                    AC

Manufactured in the United States of America
1 2 3 4 5 6 7 8 9 00 99 98 97 96 95 94 93 92 91

One summer day in the town of Zown, Mr. Lunt, the zookeeper, ran along Wheat Street waving his arms in the air. In front of the church he saw Mr. Perch, who ran the railroad.

"Have you seen my moose?" cried Mr. Lunt.

"No," said Mr. Perch. "She's not in the barn?"

"I've looked in the barn, in the yard, and all over the zoo," replied Mr. Lunt. "My moose is missing!"

"That's not all that's missing," moaned Mr. Perch, shaking his head.
"A caboose is missing from my train."
"Which caboose?" Mr. Lunt asked.
"The chartreuse caboose," said Mr. Perch. "It has disappeared."

Mr. Lunt looked at Mr. Perch. "Do you think my moose is loose in your chartreuse caboose?" he asked.

"We must search," said Mr. Perch, nodding thoughtfully.

"Time to hunt!" agreed Mr. Lunt.

They found Ms. Cook reading a book.
"Have you seen a moose on the loose in a chartreuse caboose?" they asked.

Ms. Cook stopped reading and looked up. "I saw a pig wearing a wig," she answered, "but no moose on the loose in a chartreuse caboose."

Mr. Lunt and Mr. Perch frowned.

"I'll help you look," said Ms. Cook, and she closed her book.

Mr. Wu was tying his shoe.
"Have you seen a moose on the loose in a chartreuse caboose?" they asked.

Mr. Wu looked thoughtful. "I saw a weasel paint at an easel," he said, "but no moose on the loose in a chartreuse caboose."

"We must keep looking," Mr. Lunt sighed.

"I'll help too," said Mr. Wu. "That's what I'll do."

They saw Mr. Black, who was pounding a tack.
"Have you seen a moose on the loose in a chartreuse caboose?" they asked.

Mr. Black put down his hammer and scratched his head. "I saw a bear sit in a chair," he replied, "but no moose on the loose in a chartreuse caboose."

"How will we ever find them?" cried Mr. Perch.

"I can track. I have the knack," said Mr. Black, and he joined the search.

Dr. Kale was filling a pail.
"Have you seen a moose on the loose in a chartreuse caboose?" they asked.

Dr. Kale stopped what she was doing. "I saw a goat sailing a boat," she replied, "but no moose on the loose in a chartreuse caboose."
The others looked very disappointed.
"We'll find the trail," said Dr. Kale, leaving her pail.

They met Captain Deflor, who was opening his door.
"Have you seen a moose on the loose in a chartreuse caboose?" they asked.

Captain Deflor paused. "I saw a fish making a wish," he said, "but no moose on the loose in a chartreuse caboose."

"Oh, no," groaned Mr. Lunt.

"You need one more to help explore!" cried Captain Deflor, and he closed his door to join the hunt.

Mrs. Case was running a race.

"Have you seen a moose on the loose in a chartreuse caboose?" they called to her.

Mrs. Case thought as she ran. "I saw a skunk filling a trunk," she shouted, "but no moose on the loose in a chartreuse caboose."

That was not the answer Mr. Perch wanted to hear.

"Have you any trace?" asked Mrs. Case, slowing her pace. They shook their heads, so Mrs. Case stopped running and joined the search.

They spied Miss McPeek, who was fixing a leak.
"Have you seen a moose on the loose in a chartreuse caboose?" they asked.

Miss McPeek put down her wrench. "I saw a frog out for a jog," she said, "but no moose on the loose in a chartreuse caboose."
The searchers sighed with disappointment.
"I'll help you seek," said Miss McPeek.

Professor Hugh had nothing to do.

"Have you seen a moose on the loose in a chartreuse caboose?" they inquired as they passed by.

"I saw a fox collecting rocks," he answered, "but no moose on the loose in a chartreuse caboose."

"We'll keep looking," said the others.

"A moose to pursue! I'd like something to do," thought Professor Hugh, who quickly joined them.

They hunted first in one direction and then in another, up streets and down, around corners and under stairs, but they did not find a moose on the loose in a chartreuse caboose. Hot, thirsty, and tired of searching, they all sat down on a bench in the park.

"The tracks!" shouted Mr. Black suddenly. At first no one paid attention.

"The tracks," Mr. Black repeated.

"Let him speak," urged Miss McPeek.

"The caboose runs on tracks," explained Mr. Black. "We must follow the railroad tracks."

"That's the clue," cried Professor Hugh.

"His plan can't fail," said Dr. Kale.

"I think so too," agreed Mr. Wu.

Up they all jumped and ran to the spot where the railroad tracks crossed Fleet Street. They followed the tracks in the direction that led away from the railroad yard. At the very end of the line sat the chartreuse caboose.

"Good advice we took," laughed Ms. Cook.

Inside the caboose was Mr. Lunt's moose, who was serving juice to her friend the goose.

"Hello! Would you like to join us?" asked the moose.

They all squeezed into the little caboose. The moose poured juice for everyone, and the goose passed a plate of oatmeal cookies.

"How did your caboose get here, Mr. Perch?" Dr. Kale wondered aloud. "It has no engine. It can't run by itself."

"That is true," added Mr. Wu.

Mr. Perch sipped his juice and said, "I don't know how my caboose came to be here with Mr. Lunt's moose. I'm as puzzled as you are. Does anyone know?"

"I do!" cried Professor Hugh.

"Why this place?" asked Mrs. Case.

"The tracks run downhill," explained Professor Hugh. "I think Mr. Lunt's moose, when she got loose, released the brake in the chartreuse caboose. Downhill it raced at a very fast pace, until it stopped in this space."

"It must have flown through the town, past the school and the church, stopping here with a bump and a lurch," guessed Mr. Perch.

"Quite a stunt!" said Mr. Lunt.

"But your moose is safe," said Mrs. Case.

"The caboose too!" added Mr. Wu.

"A happy ending to our search," said Mr. Perch.

"Are we all done? I had such fun! Isn't there more for us to do?" asked Professor Hugh.

"Please wait right here," Mr. Perch said. "I'll send for the engine that runs on the track and use it to pull the caboose right back. Then what we'll do is ride to the zoo!"

"A special zoo run. That will be fun!" everyone shouted.

"Invite them too," said Professor Hugh.

"Invite who?" asked Mr. Wu.

"Take a look," replied Ms. Cook. "That pig in a wig wants to join in."

"That weasel with the easel," agreed Mr. Wu, "can't wait to pursue a trip to the zoo."

"There's the bear in a chair. Let's not hold him back," urged Mr. Black.

"Take the goat on his boat," said Dr. Kale, who admired the way the goat could sail.

"That fish with a wish," declared Captain Deflor, "doesn't want to be left on the shore."

"The skunk with her trunk—let's save her a place," said Mrs. Case.

"That frog out for a jog," added Miss McPeek, "would ask to go, if he could speak."

"The fox with his rocks!" cried Professor Hugh, "He too wants to go with us to the zoo."

Into the caboose they all climbed, and the engine steamed away, straight to the gate of the Zown Town Zoo.

The moose, the goose, and everyone else climbed down the steps of the chartreuse caboose.

"This is fun! A day at the zoo!" exclaimed Professor Hugh.

"I think so too," said Mr. Wu.